INCREDIBLY CLEVER CRITTERS

A Play on Words by Patricia Poyet

Dedicated to my family

Special thanks to Aliye Çullu for her assistance
with the graphic design of this book and
to Valerie M. D'Ortona, creator of Isabel's World,
for her advice and editorial assistance.

INCREDIBLY CLEVER CRITTERS

A Play on Words by Patricia Poyet

A play on words is the clever or witty use of language so it becomes humorous or interesting.

One fine Florida day Ava and her nana spied a squirrel scampering up a tree, flicking his tail. This critter carried a nut he wanted to stash in his treasure chest. Ava's nana quipped, "That squirrel is squirreling away his nut." Ava added, "and his doughnut."

Nana thought aloud: "Animals that fly, swim, crawl, and run all have names that can be fun. If squirrels squirrel away, what can other critter names do and say? Clever critters create some amazing word play."

A search was begun for more critter fun. They looked in books, at the zoo, and on the playground, anywhere creative critters might be found.

They looked up high in the sky. They looked down low on the ground. They looked in water, under rocks, and by the seashore to find more and more critter names for their game. The names they found are within this book, so have a look.

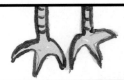

Bat

Bats bat at balloons,
making them swirl
and twirl.

Do you think they need a baseball bat?

Bug

Bug off lady bug.
Don't land on me!

Is this a grumpy bird?

Crow

A wild black crow just flew into the pumpkin patch to crow about his gold medal in front of the scarecrow and other crows.

Did the scarecrow do his job, or does he look too friendly?

Crane

Cranes crane their necks to see over the elephant to watch the circus parade. That construction crane could come in handy.

What would you lift up high
with a construction crane?

Puffin

A proud, fluffy puffin puffs up his chest as puffy clouds race by.

What makes the puffy clouds race across the sky?

Fish

A school of clownfish fish for food in pockets of coral and sea anemones.

Can you point out the sea anemones?
Hint: They are purple.

Whale

Fish have a whale of a good time atop a whale's spout in the sea near the country of Wales.

Can you find the clownfish?

Starfish

Like tiny rock stars, starfish star in a rocky tidal pool.

Do they look like bright stars shining in a dark night sky?

Worm

The bookworm worms his way into a few good books for a worm's eye view of the world.

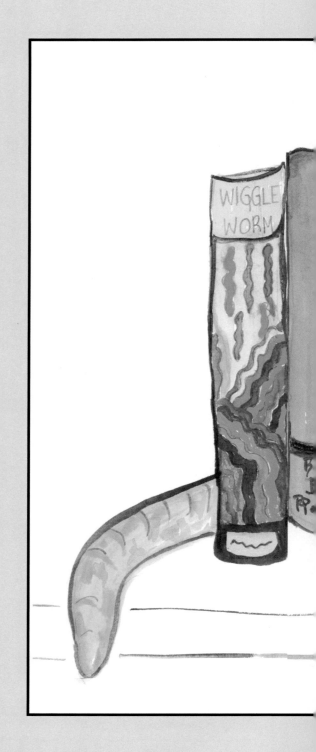

What is he reading?
Do you like his ground floor view?

Squirrel

Here is the star of this tale, Ava's squirrely squirrel, as he squirrels away nuts and doughnuts.

Where did the squirrel get his doughnuts?

Sheep

The sheep is not sheepish looking. He will protect his flock and not budge at a sheepdog's bark.

Does the sheep look wild and wooly?

Bear

The bear just grins and bears it
while he gives his friends
a boost.

Can you name the bear's animal friends?

Fox

The fox outfoxes the hounds who were hounding him by cleverly hiding in Harry Hound's doghouse instead of his own foxhole.

Can you find his foxhole?

Monkey
Horse

A monkey who paints and a painted horse seem rather silly. This creative critter must be up to monkey business.

Is the horse monkeying around, or
is the monkey horsing around?

Now that the horse has a coat of paint he might want to jump onto a merry-go-round.

Keep having FUN with animal words!

Made in the USA
Columbia, SC
15 April 2017